Searching the
Noonday
Trail

The Gun Lake Adventure Series
Book 4

by Johnnie Tuitel and Sharon Lamson

**Cedar Tree
Publishing**

SEARCHING THE NOONDAY TRAIL
Copyright 2000, 2004 by Johnnie Tuitel and Sharon E. Lamson

Published by  Cedar Tree Publishing
1916 Breton Road S.E.
Grand Rapids, MI 49506
1-888-302-7463 (toll free)

Cover and Illustration: Dan Sharp

Library of Congress Catalog-in-Publication Data
Lamson, Sharon E. 1948–
Tuitel, Johnnie, 1963–

cm.-(The Gun Lake Adventure Series)

Summary: Johnnie Jacobson starts school at the end of a busy summer and once again finds he has to prove himself. School proves to be challenging. And then a secret football play, a museum mystery and a field trip to the Chief Noonday Trail put Johnnie and his Gun Lake friends hot on the trail of another exciting adventure.

ISBN 0-9658075-3-3

[1. Adventure stories—Fiction   2. Mystery and detective stories—Fiction
3. Physically Handicapped—Children—Fiction   4. Michigan—Fiction

I. Title   II. Series: Lamson, Sharon E., 1948–, Tuitel, Johnnie, 1963–

(The Gun Lake Adventure Series)

Dedication

To my daughter Heather as you go off to college. May you search out the trails that will lead you to a fulfilling future. Remember—it's coming!

—Sharon E. Lamson

To my buddy Mac. So many years ago I dreamed I would play football like you. Watching you under the Friday night lights, I learned to love the game. Thank you, No. 22!

—Johnnie Tuitel

Meet the Gun Lake Kids

Gun Lake, Michigan is the setting for many wonderful adventures for some of the kids who live there:

Johnnie Jacobson   Eleven years old and full of adventure, Johnnie was born with cerebral palsy and uses a wheelchair to get around. He and his family moved to Gun Lake from California. The color of his dark-brown hair matches his eyes. He loves sports of all kinds—especially football.

Danny Randall   Blond, hazel eyes, and all-around sports buff, Danny loves being on the water. He is eleven years old and attends Gun Lake Middle School. With natural leadership skills and a "let's go get 'em" attitude, it's easy to see why he's Johnnie's best friend.

Katy Randall   Like her older brother, blonde-haired, green-eyed, Katy enjoys being outdoors. She also loves reading and taking care of her cat. She's nine years old and attends Chief Noonday Elementary School.

Robyn Anderson Robyn is spunky and very tall for her age—which is eleven. She likes her dark-brown hair to be kept short. She has brown eyes and tans easily in the Michigan sun. Competitive, smart and fun, Robyn enjoys being part of any adventure in and around Gun Lake.

Nick Tysman One phrase best describes ten-year-old Nick, and that is "easy going." He likes being outdoors, playing in sports and backpacking with his family out West. His brown hair and brown eyes make him look like he could almost be Johnnie's younger brother.

Joey Thomas Joey's light brown hair and hazel green eyes, coupled with his round face, make him look angelic. Openly curious about everything, Joey likes hanging out with the other Gun Lake kids. Like Katy, Joey is nine years old and attends Chief Noonday Elementary School.

Travis Hughes Travis—the picture of the perfect athlete. His sandy-blond hair, blue eyes and tanned skin make him popular with the girls. When Johnnie came into town, Travis wasn't too sure he could "hang" with someone who used a wheelchair. He and Johnnie are friends—but not close.

Acknowledgment

Thanks to George Ranville, who is of French and Ottawa-Chippewa descent, and who provided much of the research material for this book. Your enthusiasm for the Gun Lake Series and your willingness to go the second and third mile are tremendously appreciated.

Table of Contents

CHAPTER 1

Nose Tackle or Nose Dive?

"All right, now listen up!" Coach Stursma yelled. "Welcome to the IFL. We're not the NFL, we're the IFL—and we're proud of it, right?"

A chorus of "RIGHT" followed from the crowd of boys who formed a circle around Gun Lake Middle School's football coach.

"What does IFL stand for?" Johnnie Jacobson whispered to his friend Danny Randall.

"It means Intermediate Football League," Danny whispered back. Danny had to crouch in order to whisper in Johnnie's ear, because Johnnie was in a wheelchair. He had been born with cerebral palsy and, although he could stand and "walk" short distances with the use of crutches, he used his chair to get around.

"Now, as you know, there are no tryouts at this level of football," the coach continued. "But I want each of you to show me what you can do out there on the field so we'll know what position you'll play."

Just then the coach spotted Johnnie. He yelled for the

boys to run out onto the field and warm up with some laps. Then he walked over to where Johnnie was sitting. "What's your name, son?" Coach asked.

"Johnnie Jacobson, sir."

"Well, Johnnie Jacobson, sir, you can watch from over there by the bleachers." Coach pointed to the worn, wooden bleachers on the sidelines near the 50-yard line.

"I—I'm not here to watch," Johnnie stammered. "I'm here to play."

Coach Stursma looked intently at the tanned, dark-haired boy before him. He could see determination in the boy's brown eyes. He sighed. "Have you ever played football before?"

"Oh, yes sir!" Johnnie said. "When we lived in California I played."

Coach Stursma scratched his head. "Well, just how are you going to work out with the rest of the kids? We have them running laps now. I suppose you could wheel your chair around the track. But what about when the boys have to 'dance' their way through those tires out on the field? And what happens when they have to practice tackling each other?"

"Trust me, Coach. I may not be able to 'dance,' as you say, through the tires. But I can do other exercises to keep me strong and fit. If I can show you how I can get around and play nose tackle, will you give me a chance?" Johnnie asked.

The coach took off his blue and green Gun Lake Middle School Wildcats hat and smoothed back his graying and thinning hair. He gazed out at the boys who were finishing up their laps around the track, and then he looked back at Johnnie. "Well," he began slowly, "we have two weeks before school actually begins and another couple of weeks after that before we have our first game—one that is very important to our school. So, I'll be using boys who have played for me before. But if you can show me between now and when that first game starts that you can somehow be a nose tackle, then I'll consider it. Plus, I'll need a note from your parents that it's okay if you play on the team."

"Wow! Thanks, Coach! You won't be disappointed. I promise!" Johnnie said. He looked past the coach and saw Danny out on the field watching him. Johnnie gave him a thumbs-up and then proceeded to wheel himself over to the bleachers.

His friend Robyn Anderson was sitting there with Danny's sister Katy. "What's up, Johnnie?" Robyn asked. She propped her tall, thin body against the side of the bleachers. Her short brown hair was stylishly spiked.

"Coach says I can try out for the nose tackle position if I can prove myself," he answered smiling up at her.

Katy scrunched her nose and wiped a strand of her long blonde hair out of her eyes. "What in the world is a nose tackle?" she asked. "It sounds gross. Like a bunch of little noses running around and you jump on them or something."

Robyn laughed at her friend's joke. Johnnie just rolled his eyes.

"Very funny!" he said. "But a nose tackle happens to play a very important part on the defensive team. He lines up nose to nose—hence the name nose tackle—with the center on the other team. When the ball is hiked to the quarterback, the nose tackle is supposed to tackle the center so that the middle linebacker can rush through and get the quarterback."

"Whatever!" Katy said. "There are so many positions on a football team, I can never get them straight. I've heard of the quarterback and the halfback. There's probably a whole back and a piggyback too!"

Just then Danny jogged over to where the girls and Johnnie were talking. "Hi!" he said, while trying to catch his breath. "So what's the deal, Johnnie? Are you going to be on the team or what?"

Johnnie explained what the coach had said then added,

"Do you think you, me, Travis, Joey, Nick and the girls here could practice for the next couple of weeks on our own?"

"Well, I certainly don't mind," Danny said. But then he looked at the field where the other boys were still doing their running exercises, and he raised his eyebrows. "I'm not sure if Travis will want to do any extra practicing that's not going to directly help him. I guess we can ask. If he doesn't want to, there's still the rest of us!"

Travis Hughes, school jock, gave the impression he could easily grow up to become a professional football player. With his tanned skin, sun-bleached hair and deep blue eyes, he reminded Johnnie of the surfers he had seen while living in California. Travis definitely had his eyes on being the team captain this year, and Johnnie knew he wouldn't be too thrilled about taking precious time to help Johnnie become a teammate.

Just a few months ago, Johnnie first met his newfound friends, though to Johnnie it seemed like he had known them all his life. Johnnie's family had moved to West Michigan from California. Danny, Travis, Nick Tysman, Joey Thomas, Katy and Robyn were already good friends, and Johnnie was eager to get to know all of them plus his new neighborhood. In order to get into the Gun Lake "club," he had to go through an initiation. It was that adventure that not only got him into the club but also began a whole series of Gun Lake adventures throughout the summer.

But now, school was starting, and Johnnie wondered if there would be anymore excitement—besides football, of course. He, Danny, Travis and Robyn were just entering seventh grade at Gun Lake Middle School. Nick, who was ten years old, was beginning his first year in the middle school as a sixth-grader. Katy and Joey attended Chief Noonday Elementary School and would enter the fourth grade.

Johnnie watched Travis sprint through the tire obstacle. He remembered how much Travis didn't like him at first. Johnnie had to work hard to earn Travis' respect—and even now, they weren't the best of friends. But Johnnie really wanted to play football, and he knew he'd need Travis' help.

"I'd better get back to practice," Danny said. "Tell you what, I'll talk to Travis and you guys get the other kids together. Let's meet at my house this afternoon at 3 o'clock."

CHAPTER 2

Rollin' Down the Hallways

"Look! We just have one more week until school starts," Travis complained. "We've watched Johnnie do push-ups, roll around the block in his wheelchair and throw the football. Just how is all of this going to help us win a football game? How are you going to play nose tackle from your wheelchair?"

"I wasn't intending on playing nose tackle from my wheelchair," Johnnie answered.

"Really! Then what do you intend to do? Sit on the field and bite their ankles?" Travis kicked the dirt with his tennis shoe.

"Hey! That's not a bad idea!" Nick chimed in.

"Quiet, runt," Travis grumbled.

"Hey, you guys," Danny interrupted. "Knock it off. Let's just think about this a second. Johnnie's job as a nose tackle is to take down the center, right?"

"Yeah, that's the idea," Travis said.

"Well, he doesn't have to run anywhere, he just has to stop him, right?" Danny's hazel eyes were gleaming with a plan.

"What's your point, Danny?" Travis said as he paced back and forth in front of his friends.

"My point, Travis, is that I have a plan. It could be our secret weapon. Maybe not for the first couple of games, because we have to practice—*and* we have to convince Coach Stursma that it will work."

Danny shared his plan with the rest of the group. Suddenly Joey's face lit up. "Wow!" he said. "It will be so cool. Can I help Johnnie practice?"

"We can *all* help Johnnie practice—especially you, Travis. If Johnnie can successfully stop you, he can stop anyone!" Danny patted Travis on the back. "You have to admit, this could be really good!"

Travis looked down at his feet and then slowly lifted his head to look Danny square in the eyes. Slowly, he nodded his head. "Yep!" he said. "If this could work, it could be awesome!"

Every day, the kids worked on the big game plan! As practice progressed, everyone became more excited. They were convinced it would be the most unusual football play Gun Lake Middle School or anyone else, for that matter, had even seen.

ଽ

The week passed quickly. Finally the day came for school to open. "Got everything?" Johnnie's mom asked, as Johnnie wheeled into the kitchen, his backpack in his lap.

"Just need some lunch money," he answered.

"I purchased a lunch card for you," she said, handing him a plastic card. "You just slide it through the little machine next to the cash register and it deducts the amount from the money we placed in your lunch account. Be sure to keep it in your wallet!"

Mrs. Jacobson checked the time then said, "I think we'd better get you transferred into the van. We'll pick up Danny on our way, and he can show you where your homeroom is."

The ride to the school took less than ten minutes. But by the time Johnnie was lowered from the van's ramp to the sidewalk and he had secured his backpack to the back of his chair, another five minutes had elapsed.

"We better go," Johnnie said. He glanced at his watch, quickly hugged his mom goodbye and pushed himself toward the school. Danny walked beside him, ready to open the large glass doors that led into the main hallway.

Johnnie glanced back to the driveway that was in front of the school. His mother was still there, watching him go inside. She had a look on her face that let Johnnie know she was feeling a little nervous.

"Don't worry about me, Mom," Johnnie yelled back, a big grin on his face. "I'll be fine! See you this afternoon."

Danny opened the door and Johnnie pushed himself inside. Johnnie watched as his mom slowly drove away. "I hope I'll be fine," Johnnie muttered to himself.

"Your room is down this next hallway," Danny said. "Your first-hour class is English with Mrs. Walker. I hear she's pretty cool as long as you turn in your homework on time."

Danny pointed to Mrs. Walker's classroom. "I'll be by to show you where your next class is. According to your schedule here, you'll be in my math class with Mr. Hertell. See you after class."

And with that, Danny took off for his own class, leaving Johnnie parked outside Mrs. Walker's door. The halls were jammed with kids scurrying around trying to find their classes. A number of them looked at Johnnie curiously, but no one said anything.

Johnnie took a big breath and began pushing his chair inside the doorway. Just then a boy came running down the hallway and tried to squeeze through the doorway at the same time Johnnie did.

"Oof!" The boy slammed into the back of Johnnie's

chair with his stomach. He tried to move around to the side but got stuck between Johnnie's wheelchair and the door jam.

The boy's face turned beet red. "S—s—sorry," he stammered.

Mrs. Walker came to the rescue. She placed one of her feet against the wheelchair's legrests and then proceeded to pull the other boy inside the room.

"Edward," she said sternly. "If you would just get to school on time you wouldn't have to come barreling down the hallway like an out-of-control bowling ball."

"Yes ma'am," Edward said quietly. Then he turned to Johnnie and said softly, "I'm really sorry I ran into you."

It looked to Johnnie as if Edward was about to cry. "Hey, no problem," Johnnie said. "I should have waited until everyone else was inside."

"Exactly what *I* was going to say, Mr. Jacobson." Mrs. Walker raised an eyebrow. "Since you use a wheelchair, you are going to have to wait outside my classroom until everyone else is inside so you don't run into other students and they don't bump into you. Mrs. Cherup—that's our principal—told me you'd be in my class so I've arranged for you to sit up front over by the window. Will that be all right or do you have other special needs I should know about?"

Johnnie's mouth dropped open slightly. *Other needs?* he said to himself. *Gee, I don't have a disease or anything.*

But instead of saying anything, he just looked down at the floor. "The window seat will be just fine, Mrs. Walker. Sorry I caused trouble."

After class Danny waited outside the door for Johnnie. After all the other kids had left, Johnnie was permitted to leave the room.

"What gives with you being the last one out?" Danny asked. "We're going to have to hustle or we're not going to make it to class on time."

Danny got behind Johnnie's chair and began pushing it as fast as he could go. He took the turn to the connecting hallway so fast, he nearly tipped the chair over. The bell rang just as Danny wheeled Johnnie's chair into the room.

Mr. Hertell peered at the two boys from over the top of his glasses. "Glad you two could make it today," he said. Then he smiled. He looked at Johnnie. "I take it you're our new student, Johnnie Jacobson."

"Yes, sir," Johnnie said.

"And you are?" Mr. Hertell directed the question to Danny.

"I'm Danny Randall," he answered.

"Well, Danny Randall, I have placed you in the back,

second to last row. And Johnnie, I have you by the window in the front row."

"Uh, Mr. Hertell?" Johnnie said. "Could I sit in the back by the window instead? I have this, um, 'special need' with my eyesight."

Mr. Hertell picked up a stack of papers and thumbed through them. "Hmm, let's see. I don't see anything here about an eye problem. You're sure you need to sit in the *back* of the room to see better?"

"Well, I mean I *could* sit in the front, it's just that it would be better if I sat in the back," Johnnie answered.

"Very well," Mr. Hertell said. He pointed to the girl who was sitting in the window seat in the back row. "Janet? I'll need you to switch places with Johnnie here. Oh, and bring that chair with you. It appears Johnnie has brought his own."

Janet slowly shuffled toward the front of the room, dragging the chair behind her. Once she had taken her seat in the front, Johnnie carefully pushed his chair down the aisle and took his place behind the desk.

Danny, who was sitting next to him leaned over and whispered, "You don't have any trouble with your eyes! What's this 'special need' stuff?"

"Well," Johnnie whispered, "I am finding out that if I pretend to have special needs then I can sit pretty much where I want to!"

Danny rolled his eyes. "Well, don't get *too* carried away with this special needs stuff, or someone will find out that you're just playing around."

But when the end of class had just about arrived, Johnnie raised his hand.

"Yes, Johnnie," Mr. Hertell said.

"You know," Johnnie began, "it would make things a lot easier if I could leave early for my next class. And since I don't know my way around the school very well—plus it *is* kind of difficult for me to hold my books and push my chair at the same time—well, I was just wondering if I could leave five minutes early, and have another student come with me."

Mr. Hertell folded his arms and considered Johnnie's request for a moment. Then he said, "And who would you like to escort you?"

"Um, how about Janet?"

Janet, the girl who had traded places with Johnnie looked surprised, but then she smiled shyly.

"Okay, Johnnie," Mr. Hertell replied, "I guess I can comply with your request." Then turning his attention to Janet, he said, "Would that be okay with you?"

Janet smiled and shrugged her shoulders. "Sure," she said.

Danny scooted down in his seat and rolled his eyes at

Johnnie. "Now *that's* rich," he whispered. "Are you going to choose a pretty girl from *all* your classes to help you?"

"Hey! Why not?" Johnnie answered, a big smile on his face.

੨▲

Third hour, Johnnie found himself in Coach Stursma's history class with Robyn. Danny had merely pointed the way and said, "You're on your own for this one. I have to go clear across the school for gym class."

Students were filing through the door, and Johnnie patiently waited until the last one had entered the room. He pushed his way in and asked the coach where he was supposed to sit.

"Wherever you want," the coach said. "I don't believe in assigned seating. As long as you can get that chair to a desk, I don't care where you sit."

Johnnie discovered that Coach Stursma was just about the only teacher who didn't have some kind of special rule for him. Two of his teachers wanted him to leave early so he wouldn't "run over" other students in the hallway. Another one preferred that he wait until the hallways were empty. The rest didn't care when he came or left but they had their rules: Sit over here. Have someone come up to the chalkboard for you and you instruct them what to write. No hall passes unless it's an emergency, and then you will have to have someone go with you.

But the biggest rule Johnnie found both funny and irritating was the "no spaghetti" rule the cafeteria lady placed on him.

He had been going through the lunch line just fine, his tray balanced on his lap. Danny was there handing him the food he ordered. When he had ordered spaghetti, the lunch lady, Mrs. Swanson, shook her head at him. "No spaghetti for you!" she said.

Johnnie stared at her perplexed. Was she kidding? Mrs. Swanson grabbed a hamburger, plopped it on a plate and actually came around the counter to where Johnnie was waiting. She placed the plate on Johnnie's tray and wheeled him over to a side table. Then she sat next to him, and patted his head.

"Johnnie, I know you have cerebral palsy, and I just don't want you to be embarrassed. My nephew has cerebral palsy and whenever he eats something like spaghetti, it ends up all over him and all over the floor. He just can't control his hands very well, and what a mess!"

"But not all people with cerebral palsy have the same difficulties," Johnnie said. "I can't use my legs very well, and I have some weakness in my hands, but I can certainly eat spaghetti! Do you think I would have ordered it if I thought I'd make a fool of myself?"

"Just the same, I don't want to take any chances. I know this is hard for you to understand. It's nothing against you personally. Try to get over your disappointment and just enjoy your hamburger. Okay?" Mrs. Swanson patted Johnnie on the hand and stood up.

"But—" Johnnie began.

"No spaghetti!" Mrs. Swanson said. Then she shuffled back behind the counter.

"What about my lunch card?" he called out after her.

Mrs. Swanson looked at Johnnie a moment, then smiled. "Use it tomorrow!" she called back.

"I guess this means my first lunch is free!" Johnnie said, as he held his unused plastic card in his hand. "Cool!"

But the more he thought about it, the more it bugged him. He placed his lunch card in his lap and wheeled back over to the cash register.

"I really want to use my new card," he said to Mrs. Swanson. "I mean, paying for my own lunch with sort of a credit card—well, that's just kinda cool, you know?"

Mrs. Swanson laughed. "Yes, I guess you're right, Johnnie! It is cool. Go right ahead!"

CHAPTER 3

The Field Trip

Johnnie's first week at school was both frustrating and exciting. He liked his teachers but some of them bugged him a little.

"Mr. Haverkamp, my science teacher, actually came over to me after class and said if I needed any extra help with my homework, he'd be glad to work with me," Johnnie complained to his mother.

"I don't see why that should upset you," Mrs. Jacobson replied. "It sounds like he was just trying to be helpful."

"Yeah, well he said each word slowly and loudly—like I was hearing impaired or stupid—or both!"

Mrs. Jacobson sighed. "Johnnie, we both know from experience that some people think if you have a physical disability then you must have a learning disability too. Just do your homework and assignments, and soon Mr. Haverkamp will catch on that you're just as smart as the other kids in the class."

"I suppose," Johnnie said. "But you know what else? Our science class is going on a field trip to Yankee Springs Recreation Area. Some of the trails are wheelchair accessible but some aren't. So Mr. Haverkamp said I might have to sit this one out—so to speak—if the class decides to go on a trail where I can't go. I mean, *all* summer I've been water skiing, hiking in and out of the woods, using a special beach chair to get around on the sand dunes—solving mysteries. And now I may not be able to go on a field trip because the class might decide to go on a trail that's not wheelchair accessible! I mean, gee, doesn't he read the newspaper? All those adventures I've been involved in over the summer."

"Do you want me to talk to Mr. Haverkamp?" Mrs. Jacobson asked.

Johnnie sighed. "I don't know! In some ways I do, I guess. But in other ways, I don't want to be able to do things just because you talked to my teachers. You know what I mean?"

"Yes, I believe I understand." Mrs. Jacobson hesitated a moment and then said, "If there's anything I can do, let me know."

≈☙

The next day, Johnnie slowly wheeled himself into Mr. Haverkamp's science class. He was early, as usual. Mr.

Haverkamp was at the chalkboard writing out the day's assignments.

"Well, good morning Johnnie!" Mr. Haverkamp said, glancing over his shoulder. "You have quite the fan club around here!"

Johnnie's eyebrows went up in surprise. "What do you mean?" he asked.

"Yesterday, after I announced to all my science classes that we were going to take a field trip to Yankee Springs, a number of my students came up to me and wanted to make sure that wherever we went it would be wheelchair accessible so that you could go too!"

Johnnie's mouth dropped open followed by a huge smile. "Really!? Well, um, I mean, what did you decide?"

Mr. Haverkamp placed the chalk on his desk, lightly dusted off his hands and turned to face Johnnie. Then he shrugged his shoulders and smiled. "What *could* I say except that we would find a trail that's accessible! You know, I don't live in Gun Lake, but your friends filled me in on some of your big adventures this summer. I guess if you can play laser tag in the woods, go tubing behind a speed boat, camp out on a beach and go biking, then you should be able to go up and down a few hills at the recreation area. Right?"

"Right!" Johnnie answered. "Thanks, Mr. Haverkamp."

ঌ

Finally, the day of the field trip arrived. Because it was an all-day trip, the students were asked to pack a lunch and bring a snack to share. The Science Department agreed to supply beverages.

It was a warm, breezy September morning. Several busses arrived at 8 o'clock and lined up along the side of Gun Lake Middle School. Johnnie took his chair to the back of the bus. With the help of his crutches, he stood up. A parent volunteer lifted the chair and secured it in the back. Johnnie used his crutches to walk around to the side of the bus. Danny took the crutches while Johnnie used the hand rails to support himself as he climbed the steps into the bus.

"Okay, now line up according to the bus you've been assigned," Mr. Haverkamp instructed the other students. "We will have our parent volunteers onboard with you."

Danny and Robyn had already told Mr. Haverkamp that they wanted to ride with Johnnie. And Mrs. Jacobson was among the parent volunteers who went on the trip. She promised Johnnie that she would keep her distance from him but at the same time would be there if he needed her. "Thanks, Mom," he had said. "I'm really glad you're coming along!"

When the busses were loaded and all the students were

accounted for, they headed out for the relatively short ride to Yankee Springs State Park. They traveled along Chief Noonday Road to the beginning of the Chief Noonday Trail—a four-mile, hilly trail covered with asphalt and loose sand.

Once the students had gotten off the busses, Mr. Haverkamp had them form a semicircle around him. "Before we begin our four-mile hike up this trail, let me tell you what the plans are for the day. The weather couldn't be more perfect—breezy, in the 70s and blue skies.

"I have several boxes of bottled water I'll have the parents hand out in just a few minutes. Even though it's not hot and humid out, you will still be using a lot of energy going up and down the hills. And you'll need water.

"Take it slow. Look at the plant life around you. Be observant. Record in your journals what you see.

"There are about 120 of us, including parents, so I'll want to send you out in smaller groups of no more than 12 per group. We'll send the groups out in three-minute intervals. That means that the last group out will have to wait about a half hour. But not to worry. There's plenty to look at right here while you're waiting for your turn to go.

"The reason we're not going to travel as a 120-member 'herd,' is to minimize the amount we disturb the wildlife.

Remember, take it nice and easy, but don't stop for too long or the group behind you will run into you!

"The trail will lead us up to the Devil's Soupbowl, where you'll see a parking lot. For those of you who don't know what the Devil's Soupbowl is, let me explain. No one knows for sure how it happened, but that section of the park is a huge crater. We'll have to do some exploring there another time.

"Anyway, the busses will meet us there with our lunches. Then we'll grab our snacks and head out as a group to Grave Hill, up an old wagon road to Long Lake Trail. We'll cross over a bog area, where we'll do some more observing and exploring. The busses will meet us back by the Gun Lake Campground office."

Johnnie, Robyn and Danny were in the last group with Mr. Haverkamp. While they awaited their turn to go, they took a look around. Mr. Haverkamp joined them and said, "You know, this area was once the hunting grounds of the Algonquian Indians. The Algonquians were a very large tribe that lived in Canada, the Midwest, parts of the East Coast and the South. They were divided into smaller tribes called 'subtribes.' The two Algonquian subtribes that lived around here were the Ottawa and the Pottawatomie. The road we were just on and the trail we'll be exploring were named after the famous Ottawa chieftain, Chief Noonday."

"Chief Noonday?" Johnnie asked. "How did he get that name?"

"Well, his real name was Nawequageezhig," Mr. Haverkamp answered. "I guess the white settlers just translated it into an English form that was easier to pronounce and understand."

"Did the Pottawatomie live near the Ottawa Indians?" Johnnie asked.

"Well, they were neighbors," his teacher answered, "but they didn't get along very well. In fact, they had a huge battle once and fought each other using guns they had obtained from white traders. When all the fighting was over and peace was declared, the Indians gathered all the guns and threw them in the lake, where they sank to the bottom. Eventually the place became known as Penassee— or Gun Lake!"

"Wow!" said Johnnie. "I always wondered why they called this place Gun Lake."

"At some point in history, the Ottawa, Pottawatomie and another group of Indians known as the Chippewa, began using Gun Lake as a summer camp. They would set up their camps at various points around the lake, and would hunt, fish and have fun!"

"Have fun?" Robyn asked. "Somehow I don't picture Indians having fun. They always look so serious."

"Why of course they had fun!" Mr. Haverkamp laughed. "They had canoe and swimming races. This was good competition plus it enabled the young Indians to prove their strength."

&

Mr. Haverkamp continued telling them stories about Gun Lake and the Ottawa Indians. Before Johnnie knew it, the time had come for their group to start up the trail. It made it more fun to look around, knowing some of the history of the area.

The asphalt made it easy for Johnnie to push his chair. On either side were cattails, tall wild grass and small bushes. Birds fluttered by as did insects, busily gathering food. Seagulls screeched overhead.

"I'm sure glad I brought my sunblock," Johnnie said, as he rubbed some on the tops of his legs. His baseball cap offered some protection from the sun on his face.

"I hope all of you brought some insect repellant," Mr. Haverkamp said. "There are places along this trail and the one we'll be on this afternoon that are good breeding grounds for mosquitoes, gnats and other small, biting insects."

Soon the trail began climbing upward. Johnnie was having trouble pushing himself uphill, so Danny offered to help. The hill wasn't too steep, but it curved and was somewhat sandy in places. Going *down*hill, however, looked like it would be fun.

But Mr. Haverkamp warned, "Johnnie, you'd better not race down the hill in your wheelchair with all the loose sand on the trail. You could easily lose control and end up as part of the scenery."

"Aw, nuts!" Johnnie said. He had to agree, though, that it didn't look all that safe. He took it nice and slow, applying his brake when necessary, and was able to make it down every hill without toppling over or running into somebody.

By the time they reached the Devil's Soupbowl, all the other groups cheered! "Now we can eat lunch!"

While Mr. Haverkamp helped distribute all the lunches and drinks, Johnnie and the rest of his group eagerly compared notes with some of the other groups.

"We saw a beaver!" one boy exclaimed.

"Marcy here found a turtle," another boy said.

"Did you see that field of wildflowers?" a girl wanted to know.

Every group had something to share. Everyone was so busy eating and talking that the time to continue their hike came before they knew it.

Mr. Haverkamp got everyone's attention. "We're going to do this last hike as a large group. It's important that we stay together as much as possible, as there are a few stopping points along the way. I'll want to point out some interesting things to all of you.

"It would be a good idea to put on your insect repellant now, if you haven't done so already. Be sure to keep it away from your eyes and mouth. Those of you with cameras may want to take pictures of the bog area. It's really beautiful."

The five-mile Long Lake Trail wound its way through pine, oak, birch and maple trees. The old wagon road was made of dirt, and required quite a bit of effort on Johnnie's part to make it up the hills. But going downhill was a breeze, as long as he steered clear of loose rocks.

When the field trip was over, Mr. Haverkamp came up alongside Johnnie and said, "I have to admit I have been very impressed by your ability to keep up with the other students today. The trails—while easier than some of the trails in this park—are still challenging. And you've hung in there. You've gone the distance!"

Johnnie smiled. "Thanks Mr. Haverkamp. This has been a great field trip. I'd like to learn more about the Indians who lived in this area."

"Well, I happen to know that Coach Stursma is planning to take your class on a field trip to a museum where some ancient Indian artifacts are being displayed. I'm sure you'll learn a lot more about Chief Noonday and the Algonquian Indians during that field trip. And, the only thing you'll have to travel up and down on are the elevators!"

Johnnie laughed. "I'm a whiz at elevators!"

CHAPTER 4

Chieftain Necklace

"Time to get up!" Johnnie's sister Corry yelled, as she opened Johnnie's bedroom door. "Mom says you have to be at school early for your field trip. Gee, two field trips during the first couple of weeks of school. Must be rough."

Corry's dark-brown eyes sparkled with delight at having to awaken her little brother extra early. She ran a comb through her short, brown hair as she stood in the doorway watching Johnnie slowly rub his eyes. She was already dressed and ready for school. "Mom's dropping Elsa and me off at the high school a little early so she can get you to the middle school on time."

Johnnie heard his other sister Elsa protest, "If Mom would just let me get my driver's license I could take myself to school!"

She passed by Johnnie's room, then turned back and pushed Johnnie's door open wider. Her short auburn hair had a slight curl to it, which gave her an angelic look. "I hope you appreciate the extra effort it took for me to get up before the sun did just so *you* could go on your little trip," she said. Then she smiled. "And I hope you have a great time. Stay out of trouble, little brother!"

Johnnie smiled then looked at the alarm clock. He needed to be up and ready to go in just 45 minutes. But the idea of learning more about Chief Noonday and the Ottawa Indians gave him the energy he needed to get up.

His history class was taking a special trip to the museum in Grand Rapids, where a display of rare Native American pottery, jewelry and other artifacts were being shown. Most of the display came from a museum in Great Britain, which surprised Johnnie.

❧

When Johnnie arrived at the school, there were already a number of students huddled together in small groups, talking. Because the number of students who were going on this trip was small, parent volunteers agreed to transport them to the museum using their own cars and vans. Once again, Mrs. Jacobson volunteered to help out.

When all the students and drivers were accounted for, Coach Stursma ordered everyone into their vehicles. He drove the lead vehicle, and all the others followed. The trip from Gun Lake to the museum took about 30 minutes. Johnnie hardly noticed the time, because he, Robyn and a few other friends talked the whole way there.

Finally, Mrs. Jacobson announced, "We're here, everybody!"

Johnnie and his friends looked out of the van's windows. The brightly colored banners outside the Public Museum of Grand Rapids were decorated with Native American symbols. Johnnie was fascinated by the awesome size of the concrete building. Inside, he could easily see the various levels of the museum. Several huge displays were being showcased, but the most famous was the one from the British museum—namely the one that held many Indian artifacts from all over the United States, and in particular, from Michigan.

Once everyone was inside the museum, Coach Stursma was greeted by the tour guide the museum had assigned to his group. He was a medium-built man with silver hair, dressed in a gray suit. He wore a nametag but Johnnie couldn't read it from where he sat.

"Good morning!" the guide said into the microphone on his headset. He smiled at the small group of students and parents. "My name is Frank Justus, and I will be your guide today. We are going to take a brief tour of the entire museum, but our focus will be on the 'Ottawa Trails' display in the central viewing area. As you enter each display, I will give you a brief history of what you will be viewing.

Then you will be free to look around. When it's time to move to the next display, I'll make an announcement to line up by the exit door in each room. After we visit the Ottawa Trails display, you will be free to visit our museum's gift shop."

Mr. Justus turned and led the group to the first display. Johnnie found that wheeling around in the museum was a breeze compared to the trails out at Yankee Springs. He had no trouble keeping up with the rest of the group. Mr. Justus led them into a room where huge weather balloons dangled from the high ceiling. Windsocks, barometers, thermometers and other instruments used to measure atmospheric conditions lined the sides of the room. Beneath each instrument was a viewing screen that, with a touch of a button, showed how each one worked and explained what terms like "barometric pressure" meant.

The next display took them up a flight of steps. Johnnie and a few other students rode the elevator. Johnnie enjoyed the maritime display and especially liked the 10-minute video that explained the big cargo ships that sailed the Great Lakes, working their way in and out of canals and locks.

While all of the rooms were interesting, Johnnie found himself getting impatient to visit the Ottawa Trails display. Finally, Mr. Justus made the big announcement. The entire group made their way to the very top floor. Outside the entry doors were beautiful pieces of Indian pottery, furs and woven rugs. Johnnie could hear the eerie sound of drums coming from inside.

When Mr. Justus opened the doors and invited the class in, Johnnie was amazed. The room was designed to look like the area around Gun Lake he had visited just a short time ago. There was a slight breeze—probably caused by some air conditioning—and bird sounds intermingled with the drum beats. Just inside the door, a small "camp" was set up with some logs for seats, and a special screen hidden in the make-believe bushes and trees.

Mr. Justus instructed everyone to take a seat. "In a moment," he said, "we are going to see an animated video made just for this display. It will last approximately 20 minutes. Then we will continue through the forest until we come to the main display area. If you have any questions, please feel free to ask me."

Johnnie sat in his wheelchair at the end of the back row. Robyn sat beside him. The lights dimmed and the video began. A tall, Indian stood atop a hill that overlooked the Grand River and said in a deep voice, "I am Noonday, chief of the Ottawa who live here. Our people did not always live here. Our ancestors came from the north in a place now known by the white man as Ontario,

Canada. When the Europeans came to our land, they set up towns and villages and began trading along the St. Lawrence River—a river that leads from the Great Lakes to the Atlantic Ocean."

The video showed the white settlers chopping down trees and constructing stores and homes. It showed how the Ottawa people moved their own village deeper into the forest.

"While we welcomed the white men—especially the French—we wanted to farm our own land and maintain some of our own traditions. So we continued to move south into what is now called Michigan.

"Finally," Chief Noonday said, "we came to the Grand River. And here we decided to stay. While we did practice fur trading, we were basically farmers. Everyone owned the land—it belonged to the whole Ottawa tribe. We shared everything."

For 20 minutes Johnnie sat spellbound as the history of the Ottawa Indians was retold. He saw them as a peaceful people who enjoyed working the land. When white settlers came to the Grand River, they became friends with the Ottawa. The Ottawa people taught the settlers how to prepare such foods as hominy (made with corn), maple-sugar and johnny cake.

"Our people were skilled in tanning deerskin so it was

very soft and usable for making clothes. We also made beautiful feather cloaks," Chief Noonday said.

"We were considered very advanced, as we had our own written language made up of detailed pictures that told a story. We also used fish, shells and ashes to fertilize our fields, plus we made spades and hoes to work the land."

When the video was over, Johnnie and Robyn headed back out to the path that led them past Ottawa farms. There was a likeness of a small Ottawa boy collecting maple sap. Even women helped gather food. They would wade into the water and "walk" the fish toward the shore, where other Ottawa would scoop them out of the water.

"This forest is so real!" Johnnie whispered to Robyn. "I wonder if there are any mosquitoes in here."

Robyn chuckled. "Hey! Looks like we're heading into an Ottawa house!" she said. They opened the door and went inside, only to find themselves in the main display hall. Other visitors were there too.

"Wow!" Johnnie exclaimed. "Look at the jewelry and beadwork."

"And look over here," Robyn said, pointing to a tall likeness of Chief Noonday. "It's the big chief himself! And—oh! Come here and take a look at this!"

Johnnie pushed himself over to where Robyn was practically jumping up and down. "Look! Can you believe that Chief Noonday actually wore that?"

Robyn pointed to a large copper pendant, which hung from a beautifully decorated strip of cloth. The pendant was engraved with a delicate pattern. It hung majestically around the tall chief's neck and down midway to his waist. His arms were folded against his chest, and he looked wise and serene.

"I wonder if he was really that tall," Robyn said.

Mr. Justus had just stepped up behind Robyn and Johnnie. "Yes, we believe he was," he said. "The Ottawa were tall and very well built."

"Was he taller than most of the other Ottawa?" Johnnie asked. "Is that why he became chief?"

"I don't think size had much to do with it," Mr. Justus answered. "To be a chief, you had to be brave, strong, generous and wise. Then you had to encourage your people to develop the same qualities. Good chiefs, like Chief Noonday, led their people by example."

"Was he the most famous Ottawa chief?" Robyn asked.

"Well, most people remember Chief Pontiac who came before Chief Noonday. When the English settlers fought the French and won, back in 1760, the English thought they could best control the Indians by making very harsh rules and punishments. For example, they would stop sending supplies that the Indians needed if they didn't do what the English wanted them to. Needless to say, the Indians didn't like that very much. The Seneca tribe tried to stand up to the English, but none of the other tribes would cooperate. They weren't very well organized.

"But then one day, an Ottawa Indian named Pontiac became chief. They say he looked like a fierce warrior. And he could speak very well and convincingly. Besides all of that, he knew how to get all the tribes working together. He could envision a future for his people, plus he had fought with the French against the British, so he knew he could count on the French settlers to help his cause.

"Many other tribes respected Pontiac, and he talked to them about being unified. But he also stressed the importance of being friends with the French and using guns. With his help, the Ottawa became established in the area."

"Wow!" said Robyn. "Isn't that fascinating, Johnnie?"

Just then the lights flickered and went out. The room was dark, except for some filtered light coming in from the windows. A few moments later, they flickered back on.

"Hmm, must be that construction that is going on down the street," Mr. Justus said. "Yesterday a truck hit a power line, and the same thing happened."

Johnnie was strangely silent. He looked around and

then headed over to another display. Robyn walked over and stood beside him.

"Are you okay?" she asked.

"Yeah, sure! Why?" he replied.

"Well, you just sort of rolled away after Mr. Justus told us about Chief Pontiac."

"Oh! I wasn't upset, I just—well, I just wanted to come over here and see this stuff," he said, pointing to the pottery. "Hey! Looks like everyone's getting ready to go down to the gift shop. Let's get in line," Johnnie said. He rolled quickly away from Robyn and joined the other students. Then he looked back at Robyn and motioned for her to get in line too.

Robyn shrugged her shoulders. "Oh well!" she said to herself. "*Something's* up with Johnnie, but I guess I won't be able to find out what it is—yet!"

She smiled to herself. If Johnnie Jacobson thought he was going to hide something from Robyn, he had another thought coming.

CHAPTER 5

News Flash!

"Look! If you want my help, then you are going to have to snap out of this mood you're in and come to our special football practices," Travis said. He stared hard at Johnnie, who slouched down in his wheelchair and seemed to be on another planet.

Danny shook Johnnie's shoulders. "He's right, Johnnie. You wanted to prove to the coach that you could play nose tackle but you don't seem to want to practice with us. How are we going to perfect our secret play without *you*?"

Just then Robyn bounded into the Jacobson's backyard. "Hey! What gives? The rest of us have been waiting for a half hour. Are we going to play football or what?"

"Looks like it's going to be 'or what'," Danny said. "Johnnie just doesn't seem to want to do anything."

Robyn squatted in front of Johnnie's chair. "Does this have anything at all to do with our field trip to the museum?" she asked, looking directly into his eyes. "Because if it does, then you'd better tell us what the big problem is so we can get on with football practice."

Johnnie frowned and pushed Robyn back. She nearly landed on her backside but she caught herself. "I just don't want to practice," he said. "That's all."

"Well, Coach Stursma said he was coming over to watch us do our stuff," Danny said. "I guess, we'll just have to tell him that without you, there's not much to see."

Johnnie started to say something but then closed his mouth and stared at the ground.

Danny sighed. "C'mon, let's go back and tell the others that practice is off." He motioned for Travis and Robyn to follow him.

Johnnie watched them go. He bit his lip and hit the arm of his wheelchair with his fist. "Go ahead," he muttered to himself. "I don't care."

❧

Johnnie was still sitting in the backyard of his house when his mother came out. "Johnnie," she said softly. "There's someone here who would like to talk to you."

He looked up only to see Coach Stursma standing beside his mother.

"I'll leave the two of you alone to talk," she said, as she made her way back into the house.

Coach Stursma grabbed one of the lawn chairs and brought it over next to Johnnie's chair. He sat down and looked up into the sky. Some geese were flying in formation overhead, honking loudly as they glided through the air.

"So why are you here?" Johnnie asked, after a few moments of silence had passed.

"Well," Coach began, "I went out to watch you practice today, but you weren't there. The kids told me you're giving up football. Is that correct?"

Johnnie avoided looking at his teacher. "Well, yeah— I mean, I guess so. I don't know."

"Robyn told me that something happened at the museum that changed your whole attitude. Want to talk about it?" Coach Stursma looked directly at Johnnie.

Johnnie's breathing became faster and he grabbed the armrests of his wheelchair, his knuckles turning white. He felt like he was going to explode. Suddenly, he jerked his wheelchair so that he faced away from his teacher.

"It's just—" he began. "I mean, well, I—what I'm trying to say is that I will never be a chief," Johnnie stammered.

Coach Stursma scratched his head. "Johnnie, please turn around and look at me," he said. "What are you talking about?"

Johnnie took a deep breath and slowly turned his chair around so that he faced his coach.

"The tour guide was telling us all about the Ottawa chiefs. He said that in order to be a chief, a person had to be brave and strong. Chief Pontiac looked like a fierce warrior and even fought in battles. Chief Noonday was a tall and powerful man. If *I* had been born an Ottawa, I never would have been a chief. And I got to thinking that I'll probably never be a good leader—or a good football player—or a good anything."

Coach Stursma nodded his head. "Well, Johnnie, you're right about some things and wrong about some things. You're right that you probably never would have been an Ottawa chief. But you have to remember, people didn't understand or think about disabilities the way we do now. Back then, they didn't have the medical know-how we have today—or even wheelchairs! Chances are, you wouldn't have survived very long.

"But as for being a good leader—well, Franklin Delano Roosevelt was one of the presidents of the United States, and he used a wheelchair. He may not have fought in any wars, but he was the leader—or chief—of our country."

"Yeah, but he hid his disability," Johnnie said. "He thought people wouldn't respect him if they knew he couldn't walk like other people."

"You're right about that, Johnnie," Coach Stursma answered. "But in the years since Roosevelt was president, people have come to understand disabilities better. That's why it was finally decided to make a statue of Franklin Roosevelt sitting in his wheelchair. People are beginning to understand that just because someone can't walk or see or hear, doesn't make him or her an incomplete person.

"Franklin Delano Roosevelt had polio, which affected his legs. Beethoven wrote beautiful pieces of music and entire symphonies, yet he had a hearing impairment. Helen Keller could neither see nor hear, but with help from her teacher, she learned sign language and was later very helpful to many people. And what about Frank Dempsey of the New Orleans Saints. He only had half a foot, yet he used it to kick a 63-yard field goal—the longest in NFL history!

"Johnnie—you of all people know that there are athletes who have legs missing who still run marathons and jump hurdles. There are people in wheelchairs who play an awesome game of basketball or tennis—and many of them dedicate themselves to helping others who have disabilities. What about all those adventures you told me you experienced over the summer?"

Coach leaned back in the chair and smiled. "Just because you can't be an Ottawa chief means you're going to give up on life?" Then he leaned forward and looked intently at Johnnie, who was now looking down. "Besides," he continued, "you're Dutch not Ottawa!"

Johnnie felt a smile creep across his face. Then he let out a short little laugh.

Coach Stursma stood up and Johnnie looked at him in the face for the first time that afternoon. "I'm going to be stopping by your neighborhood tomorrow afternoon," Coach said. "I am hoping I'm going to see some pretty awesome football plays."

He smiled at Johnnie and gave him a pat on the head. Then he walked around the side of the house to the driveway. Mrs. Jacobson came out the backdoor just as Coach Stursma drove off down the street. "Feeling better?" she asked.

"Yeah," he said. "I guess I'd better call Danny and the rest of them and apologize. Then I'll see if they still want to practice tomorrow."

❧

Later that evening, the Jacobsons settled in front of the television set to watch the nightly news. Warren Reynolds of WOOD TV reported that the Public Museum of Grand Rapids had been robbed. He said that among the items reported missing was the copper necklace that had hung around the statue of Chief Noonday.

Other items missing were various jewelry pieces, pottery and woven rugs.

"Why that happened while *we* were there!" Mrs. Jacobson exclaimed. "I sure didn't see anything, and we were there almost the entire day."

"I can't believe they took Chief Noonday's necklace!" Johnnie said. "Why would anyone take a necklace? Is it worth a lot of money or something?"

"Well, as a matter of fact, it is!" Mr. Jacobson said. "And to some people, it's worth more than money."

"Huh?" Johnnie said. "How can something be worth more than money?"

"How much is your health worth to you?" Mr. Jacobson asked. "Would you sell your good health for money? And what about your family or your Dutch heritage? How much money are they worth?"

"Oh, I get it," Johnnie said. "So you think that someone took those things because they were of value to them—other than money?"

"Well, I really don't know why those things were stolen," Mr. Jacobson admitted. "But I'm just saying it could be for reasons other than just money. However, those things *are* worth a lot of money—and we know that the love of money is the root of all evil."

❧

The next day at school, everyone was talking about the museum robbery. As Johnnie wheeled himself into Coach Stursma's history class, he noticed a man wearing a suit and tie talking to his teacher. The bell rang, and all the students found their seats. Because the stranger was in the room, they quieted down quickly.

"Class," Coach Stursma said, "this is Detective Knoll. He would like to talk to you for a few minutes before we begin class."

Detective Knoll stood in front of Coach Stursma's desk. He was a short, balding man, with small dark eyes that seemed to dart around the room as he spoke. "As you know, the Ottawa Trails display was robbed. We figure it was about the same time your class was there," he said. He paused and looked grimly around the room. "From what I understand, the boy in the wheelchair—"

"His name is Johnnie Jacobson," Coach Stursma said, interrupting the detective.

"Yes, well, Johnnie Jacobson was one of the last people to view the necklace before the group exited the room," Detective Knoll said.

He looked directly at Johnnie and said, "Now, I realize that *you* couldn't have taken the necklace, but I was wonder—"

"What do you mean I *couldn't* have taken the necklace?" Johnnie shouted. "You think that just because I'm in a wheelchair I'm helpless? I could have easily stood up and hung onto the statue." Johnnie demonstrated that he could stand by hanging onto the desk in front of him.

"Maybe I *did* take it and put it into my backpack!" Johnnie was getting louder.

"Did you take it?" Detective Knoll asked calmly.

"I didn't say that I *took* it, only that I *could* have taken it if I had wanted to," Johnnie answered.

"Well, maybe we should take a look inside your backpack just to make sure," the detective stated.

"What?! You think I really *did* steal that necklace?" All of a sudden, Johnnie realized that he had made himself look suspicious.

"Johnnie," Coach Stursma began, as he walked over to Johnnie's desk, "No one is accusing you of anything. Just calm down!"

"No!" Johnnie shouted. "I can easily prove my innocence." With that, he took his backpack and dumped the contents on his desk.

Suddenly, a gasp escaped from Robyn's mouth, for there on Johnnie's desk, in plain view, was Chief Noonday's necklace.

CHAPTER 6

Surprises Come in Twos!

Johnnie found himself sitting outside the principal's office, waiting for his parents to join him. Detective Knoll was in the office with Coach Stursma and the school principal, Mrs. Cherup. Johnnie felt numb. *How did that necklace get into my backpack?* he wondered.

While he thought about what he was doing when he was in the big display room at the museum, and who could have put the necklace into his backpack, which was hanging off the back of his chair, his parents arrived.

"Johnnie!" His mother looked like she was going to cry. "What on earth has happened? How did that necklace get into your backpack?"

"What has the detective said so far?" his father wanted to know.

Before Johnnie could answer, the door to the principal's office opened. "Won't you all come in?" Mrs. Cherup said.

Detective Knoll was standing on one side of Mrs.

Cherup's desk. He watched Johnnie and his bewildered parents enter the room.

After Mrs. Cherup closed her office door and took a seat behind her desk, Detective Knoll walked over toward Johnnie and said, "Even though you demonstrated how you *could* have stolen the necklace, I believe you were as surprised at finding it in there as we were! Of course, I'll have to send the necklace to the lab to check for fingerprints. When you dumped out the contents of your backpack, I didn't see you pick up the necklace, so there shouldn't be any of your prints on it, right?"

Johnnie nodded. Then Mr. Jacobson interrupted. "Detective, are you saying you don't think Johnnie took the necklace?"

"What I'm saying," Detective Knoll said, "is that it doesn't seem likely. However, I'm not ruling out anything until I get the results back from the lab. Unfortunately, that means Johnnie will have to come down to the station and be fingerprinted."

Mrs. Jacobson started sniffling, and Johnnie felt horrible.

"Don't feel too badly about being fingerprinted," the detective said. "Many parents have their children fingerprinted—as a safety precaution."

It wasn't the fingerprinting that bothered Johnnie. It was his mother's crying.

"I'm sorry, Mom. I really am," he said.

"Oh, honey! I don't blame you one bit," she said, while dabbing at her eyes. She managed a weak smile. "Crying is just one way for me to work off some stress."

"If you don't really suspect that Johnnie did it," Coach Stursma said, "then is he free to attend classes and football practice?"

"Of course!" Detective Knoll said. "On the other hand, I would ask that he not leave town until the lab reports come back. And if we could take a quick trip down to the police station, we can get this fingerprinting over with in just a few minutes."

"Well, I guess everything's settled—at least temporarily," Mrs. Cherup said.

"Not quite," said Detective Knoll. "Coach Stursma, if you or any of your students saw anything that was suspicious, please let me know. We're going to take a look at the surveillance tapes from the museum, this afternoon. Hopefully, they will show us what happened."

Johnnie and his parents left the room. "Are you feeling okay about finishing out the day at school?" his mother asked.

"Yeah," Johnnie said. "I'm just glad he doesn't think I really did it."

❧

After Johnnie returned from the police station, the rest of the day went fairly well. Of course all his friends had heard about it and were dying to know what had happened in the principal's office.

Danny caught up with Johnnie during the last class of the day. "You're not arrested or anything like that, are you?" Danny asked. "I mean, we're still on for football practice, aren't we?"

Johnnie smiled. "Yep! We're still on, as long as we don't practice in Ohio, or someplace like that!"

Johnnie laughed at the puzzled look on Danny's face. "I was told not to leave town," he explained.

"Oh!" Danny said. Then he laughed with relief. "I couldn't imagine why we'd practice in Ohio!"

ə♠

After school, Johnnie's friends met him at the park across the street from the school. There was a large baseball field that they decided to use for practice.

Travis stood facing his friends and said, "First, we have to do some warm-ups before Coach gets here. Johnnie, there's an asphalt walking path that circles the baseball field. Go do a couple laps around that."

"Hey! Danny!" Johnnie called. "I forgot to ask my mom to drop off my crutches. Can you call her from the school?"

"No problem!" Danny yelled from the other end of the field. And he ran off toward the school.

"Crutches?" Katy asked. "Don't tell me you're going to tackle people with your crutches!"

"No, not exactly," Johnnie said, as he headed toward the walking path. "Just wait, you'll see."

"This is going to be so cool," Nick said. "I don't know what he's going to do, but it's going to be excellent and really fun to watch."

After about fifteen minutes, Johnnie had completed his warm-up. Just then his mom pulled up in the van, with his crutches. "You be careful out there, Johnnie!" she yelled from the van. Danny ran over to where she was parked and retrieved the crutches. "You know how I feel about football," she called out. "Your father may think it's a good idea, but I'm not too sure. Maybe you could be the team manager!"

Johnnie sighed. "Thanks for the crutches, Mom!" he shouted from the baseball field. "I'll see you later!" He waved, letting his mom know he didn't want to talk about the "evils" of football right then.

"Okay," Travis said, as Mrs. Jacobson slowly drove off, "let's practice our secret move before Coach Stursma gets here. I want us to at least *look* like we know what we're doing.

"Danny, you be the quarterback and I'll be the center. Nick, you and Joey line up on either side of Johnnie, who is the nose tackle. Robyn and Katy you are receivers."

Before they could get the play off, Coach Stursma jogged over to where they were practicing. "Hold up there a moment," he yelled. Then when he reached them, he said, "I've only got a few moments before I have to go, so quick show me what you have in mind."

"We haven't had time to really practice it yet," Travis said. "We're not even sure it's going to work."

"Look, our first game is tomorrow," Coach said, "and I have to get back across the street to warm-up the team. Tell you what, practice this secret play of yours for awhile, and *maybe*—if it's good enough—I'll let you play in the second game, which is a week away."

He noted the disappointed look on Johnnie's face. "Hey," Coach said, "I'm giving you a fair chance. You say you're not ready, so I'm giving you more time."

"Oh, I agree," Johnnie said. "I just wish I could play in the first game. But I'll be more than ready for the second!"

As soon as Coach left, Travis and Danny had to leave too, so they could practice with the rest of the team. "We'll meet you later, after supper," they called to Johnnie. "Then we'll really start practicing our secret move," Danny yelled back over his shoulder.

❧

Robyn and Katy walked home with Johnnie. Mrs. Jacobson greeted them at the front door. "Want to come in for some cookies and lemonade?" she offered.

"No thanks, Mrs. Jacobson," Robyn said. "I've got some homework to do before dinner."

"Me too," Katy said. "See you after dinner, Johnnie!"

After the girls had left, Mrs. Jacobson helped Johnnie get inside the house. "It sure has been an unusual day!" she said. "First we get a call from the school, and then I find out you're trying out for the football team. You *do* have a permission slip for me to sign, don't you?"

"Coach says you just have to sign a note," Johnnie answered.

"I'm not so sure I want you playing football," Mrs. Jacobson said.

"Mom, I played football in California. And I never got hurt once. Well, I never got *seriously* hurt!"

"A broken ankle wasn't serious?" Mrs. Jacobson asked, raising one eyebrow.

"Well," Johnnie said, as he wheeled into the kitchen to grab a cookie, "it wasn't serious to me! I never could stand very well on that ankle anyway!"

"Ha! Ha!" Mrs. Jacobson said, trying to hide a smile. "That's very funny!"

❧

That night after dinner, Johnnie and his sisters were clearing the table when the telephone rang. Mr. Jacobson answered it. Johnnie could tell from his father's side of the conversation, that he was most likely talking to either Detective Knoll or some other policeman.

"Thank you!" Mr. Jacobson said. "I'm sure he'll be greatly relieved."

Mr. Jacobson looked at Johnnie as he replaced the phone on its cradle. "That was Detective Knoll, and guess what?"

"My fingerprints weren't on the necklace!?" Johnnie replied.

"Not only that," Mr. Jacobson said, "that wasn't even the *real* necklace!"

"What?" Mrs. Jacobson exclaimed. "It was a fake?"

"Yep! That's what the lab reports and the museum officials have determined. Johnnie, you're definitely off the hook."

"Yes!" Johnnie said. "I *knew* I was innocent."

Everyone laughed.

"By the way, Detective Knoll said we weren't to talk to anyone about the fake necklace. Oh! And one more interesting fact," Mr. Jacobson continued. "The video surveillance tapes were blank for a short period of time—almost like someone got a hold of them and erased part of it."

"So they couldn't see who took the necklace?" Johnnie asked.

"The tapes showed nothing." Mr. Jacobson scratched his head. "I wonder who would have access to the video camera?"

"Wait a minute!" Johnnie cried. "There was a short blackout just before we left the exhibit hall. Remember, Mom?"

"Why yes! I *do* remember the lights flickering and then blinking off for a few moments," she said.

"The tour guide said the lights had done that the day before too. He blamed it on some construction truck hitting the power line. Maybe when the lights went out, the cameras stopped working too," Johnnie said.

"Hmm," said Mr. Jacobson. "I think you may have something there. We'll call Detective Knoll in the morning and let him know."

CHAPTER 7

Nathaniel Noonday

The day of the big football game finally arrived. The weatherman promised that it would be a mostly sunny day, with little chance of rain. Johnnie rolled into his first-hour English class a little ahead of the other students. Mrs. Walker was looking over her lesson plan when he arrived.

"Good morning, Johnnie," she said, glancing up at him.

"Good morning, Mrs. Walker," Johnnie replied, as he took his place behind his desk. He opened his backpack and retrieved the homework he had done.

Then he gazed out the window. He heard the other students shuffle in but his mind was on two things—first, the game that afternoon, and second, the fake necklace.

Johnnie managed to pull his attention back to class but for some reason, he couldn't wait until his third-hour history class with Coach Stursma. He wanted to find out if Coach Stursma had heard about the fake necklace yet.

Johnnie tried hard to focus on both his English and

math classes, and when the bell rang, signaling the end of his second-hour class, he raced out of the room and headed toward Coach Stursma's classroom. He was traveling full speed when Mrs. Cherup walked around the corner. At the sight of Johnnie barreling down the hallway straight at her, she jumped back against the lockers.

"Johnnie Jacobson!" she said loudly.

At the sound of his name being called, Johnnie brought his chair to a quick halt. When he saw it was Mrs. Cherup, his heart sank.

She walked over to him and placed a hand on one of her hips. Her bright blue eyes bore into him. With a frown she demanded, "Just what do you think you are doing using our hallway as a race course?"

"I—I'm sorry, Mrs. Cherup," Johnnie replied. "I guess I was so excited about getting to my history class that I wasn't thinking." He looked up pleadingly at her.

"Why are you so excited about history?" Mrs. Cherup asked. But before Johnnie could reply, she added, "Is it history or could it be the visitors you have in class today?" She smiled at him and then said, "Slow down, Mr. Jacobson—and watch out for who you might be running over!"

Mrs. Cherup patted the back of Johnnie's wheelchair, then she took off down the hall.

"Visitors?" Johnnie said to himself. "I wonder who they could be?"

He hurried, as fast as he dared, to the classroom. When he finally wheeled himself inside, he saw Coach Stursma talking to three young men. Johnnie guessed they were college-age. The tallest one had straight black hair, held back by an elastic band into a neat ponytail. He was wearing black slacks and a deep purple business shirt with a matching silk tie. The other two were similarly dressed with dark slacks and color-coordinated shirts and ties. They both had dark-brown hair. One wore his sort of spiked, while the other one had his hair parted on one side.

When Johnnie entered the room, the tallest one saw him and stopped talking. Coach Stursma turned around and, spotting Johnnie, said, "Johnnie, I'd like to introduce you to Jake Smith, Trevor Dubois and," he said, pointing to the tallest, "Nathaniel Noonday."

"Nathaniel *Noonday*!" Johnnie exclaimed. "As in *Chief* Noonday?"

Nathaniel smiled. "Well, *I'm* not Chief Noonday, but he was my great-great-great-great-*great* grandfather."

"Wow!" Johnnie said. "Do you live around here?"

"No, actually, I live in Tennessee. My friends and I are just visiting. We read about my ancestor's necklace being displayed at the museum in Grand Rapids, and so we decided to check it out!"

Johnnie scrunched his nose and sat back in his chair. "You mean to tell me that you drove here *all* the way from Tennessee just to see some necklace?"

Nathaniel laughed. "I know it sounds ridiculous, doesn't it? But actually, the British Museum has quite a number of Ottawa artifacts that we were anxious to see. Many of us believe these artifacts should be returned to the United States, but there are no laws that support our view. So, we decided to make the trip to Michigan and at least take pictures.

"Then we found out that the necklace had been stolen, and that you and your classmates were at the museum the day it disappeared."

"But—" Johnnie began.

Coach Stursma moved in front of Johnnie and said, "No more talking for now..."

"But Coach, the necklace!" Johnnie persisted.

Coach raised an eyebrow and said quietly but sternly, "It's time for you to get to your seat. Mr. Noonday and his friends have agreed to tell us some of the stories they learned about their people."

"I just wanted to tell them..."

"Johnnie!" Coach Stursma pointed toward the back of the room.

Slowly, Johnnie pushed his wheelchair back to his desk. Coach Stursma followed him, scribbling some notes on a piece of paper as he walked. He placed the folded paper on Johnnie's desk. Johnnie looked at him questioningly, but Coach Stursma pretended not to notice.

As Coach Stursma moved to the front of the class to introduce everyone to their guests, Johnnie unfolded the note. It read, "No one is to know about the fake necklace."

Johnnie quickly refolded the note and stuck it in his pocket. *That's weird,* Johnnie thought. *I wonder why no one is supposed to know that the necklace they found in my backpack wasn't the real one?*

As Johnnie pondered the mystery, Nathaniel Noonday began talking about his ancestor, Chief Noonday. "One day, the chief was in the river with a white man," Nathaniel said. "It looked as if they were wrestling. All of a sudden, the white man whose name was Reverend Leonard Slater, leaned over the tall chief and pushed him down into the water. At that moment, many of the Indians who were watching from the banks of the river called out, *Yahi tah yal, kitchee mokomon!* That is Ottawa for, 'Hurrah, hurrah, the white man got him down first!' They didn't realize that Reverend Slater was actually *baptizing* Chief Noonday as part of a religious ceremony. That happened sometime during the summer of 1827."

Janet, who was sitting in the front row, raised her hand. "Why did Chief Noonday change his religion?"

Nathaniel smiled. "He wanted the white people to know that the Ottawa were serious about being part of the white world. He knew the old ways had to end, and he wanted his people to be in a better position to receive all the goods the white man was bringing from Europe."

"So he didn't *really* become a Christian?" Melissa asked.

"Actually, he did," Nathaniel said. "He lived in the area for awhile and then left. No one knows what actually happened to him after 1852, but many Ottawa moved south. There's a group of Christians in Georgia who belong to the Noonday Baptist Association. I don't know for sure, but it sounds like some of my ancestors remained Christians and established churches in the south."

Nathaniel told many other interesting stories for the rest of the hour. Everyone was spellbound when suddenly the bell rang, signaling the end of class.

"Well thank you very much for sharing part of your history with us," Coach Stursma said. "I understand you'll be around town for a few days. Perhaps you'd like to watch our football game this afternoon!"

"That would be awesome!" Nathaniel said. Then he and his friends left.

Coach Stursma handed out some papers. "These are your study guides for the test that will be on Friday. And, Johnnie, would you mind staying after class a few minutes?"

Johnnie nodded his head. *What's going on now?* he wondered.

≈

After class was dismissed, Coach Stursma said, "Johnnie, I'm sorry I had to cut you off like that when you were talking to Nathaniel Noonday. But Detective Knoll made it very clear that they don't want people to know that the necklace they found was a fake—at least, not yet. Someone still has the real one!"

"I guess I understand," Johnnie said. "But then people will think I stole it!"

Coach shook his head. "Detective Knoll assured me he was making a statement to the press that would clear you of any wrongdoing. He said he'd tell them your fingerprints were not on the necklace and that they suspect someone put it there, which, of course, is what happened."

"Yeah," Johnnie said. "But who and why?"

CHAPTER 8

I Spy

Busses from the rival school arrived at 3:45 p.m. Johnnie wheeled himself over to the stands on the "home" side. Robyn, Katy, Nick and Joey joined him. As students found their way to bleacher seats, Johnnie spotted Nathaniel Noonday and his friends coming toward him. They had changed into more casual clothes.

"Hey, Johnnie!" Nathaniel said. "Mind if we sit with you?"

"No, I don't mind," Johnnie answered. Then he introduced the rest of his friends.

Both teams were out on the field doing some warm-ups. "I've only visited this area once before, when I was a boy," Nathaniel said. "There are many places here at Gun Lake that the Ottawa considered to be sacred."

"Really?" Johnnie said. "I just moved here from California early this summer, so I really don't know much about this place either."

"Hmm. Well, maybe we can do some exploring this weekend," Nathaniel suggested. "Perhaps some of your friends would like to come along."

"Wow! That would be great!" Johnnie said.

"By the way, I heard that they found the necklace of Chief Noonday in your backpack," Nathaniel said. "Are you in any trouble over that?"

"No. My fingerprints were not on the necklace. They think someone else put it in there," Johnnie said.

Nathaniel gazed out at the football field then said, "From what I understand, it was a fake anyway."

Robyn overheard what Nathaniel had said. "What?!" she said. "Excuse me for listening in, but did you say the necklace in Johnnie's backpack was a fake?"

"Uh," Nathaniel stammered. "Well, that's what I heard anyway. What did the police tell you, Johnnie?"

Johnnie remembered what Coach Stursma had said— that no one was supposed to know the necklace wasn't the real one. He didn't want to lie but he didn't want to betray a confidence either, so he said, "The police didn't tell me anything." *After all,* Johnnie reasoned with himself, *it wasn't the police who told me, it was my dad!*

Just then, the announcer stated that the game was about to begin. Players from the visiting team were greeted, and then the Gun Lake Wildcats came out on the field, amidst the excited cheering of the fans.

A coin was tossed, and it was determined that the Wild-cats would receive the ball. Travis was the team's starting quarterback and Danny was a wide receiver. The other team, the Grand Valley Warriors, sent their kick-off team out onto the field. They kicked the ball—a nice high, arch-ing kick—and the Wildcats' receiver caught it and began running a zigzag pattern back toward the Wildcat goal. He got to about the 40-yard line before he was tackled.

Nathaniel watched Johnnie for a few moments. "You really get into football, don't you?" he asked.

"Oh yes!" Johnnie replied, his eyes not leaving the field. "I'm planning on playing nose tackle in the next game."

Nathaniel raised his eyebrows in surprise. Johnnie caught the look out of the corner of his eye and said, "Oh, I know I don't *look* like I could play football, but don't let this wheelchair fool you. We have a secret play that's go-ing to be awesome! I'm hoping to try it out next week."

"I wish I could stick around until next week to see it," Nathaniel said.

"Hey, look!" Katy yelled. "There's Danny!"

Danny was at the far end of the field, lined up against the defense. When the center snapped the ball back to Travis, who was the quarterback, Danny began running up the field toward the sideline. Travis saw him and threw the ball. It was a little high, but Danny jumped for it and managed to catch it. Once he landed on the ground, he began running toward the goal. The other team ran toward Danny, intent on stopping him.

"Run! RUN!" Katy and Robyn screamed.

Joey and Nick were standing up yelling, "Go, go, go!"

Danny ran for about 10 yards before he was tackled, but the play had gained them about 20 yards. They were now across the 50-yard line.

"I confess, I don't know too much about football," Nathaniel said. "Which position on the field is the one you want to play?"

"See how the teams are lining up on the field?" Johnnie said. "The team that has possession of the ball is the offensive team. The front line of players on the offensive team is called the offensive line. The guy with the ball right now is the center. He'll snap the ball back to the quarterback who will either throw it or give it to a player who will run with it.

"Now, see the other team? That's the defense. The front line of players facing the offensive team is called the defensive line. See the guy in the middle, right across from the center? That's me! Or, it will be next week—I hope!"

"What's his main job?" Nathaniel asked.

"His main job is to help the defensive line take down

the offensive line so the other defensive players can get to the quarterback or the other running backs—players who the quarterback would give the ball to."

"Those guys look pretty big!" Nathaniel remarked.

"Yeah, they usually are. In the pros, there was this guy called William Perry who played defense for the Chicago Bears. His nickname was 'Refrigerator' because he was so big. He weighed about 360 pounds—and not too many players got past him!"

Nathaniel laughed. "I guess not! Now, no offense Johnnie, but you don't look like you weigh anywhere near 360 pounds!"

Johnnie smiled and slowly turned to look at Nathaniel. "It's not always size that counts," he said. "It's how you use what you've got!"

Nathaniel gazed admiringly at Johnnie. "You know, you're all right," he said.

❧

It was now the fourth quarter and the score was Wildcats 14; Warriors 17. The Warriors had the ball. "Come on!" Johnnie yelled. "Defense! Defense! Sack the quarterback. Do *something*!"

"Calm down," Robyn said. "Our guys are doing the best they can."

"Yeah, well if *I* were out there..." Johnnie didn't finish

his sentence because the play was underway. The Wildcat's defense held up well but the Warrior's quarterback, sent the ball spiraling to one of his receivers, who caught it and ran out of bounds. That gave the Warriors a first down, and the right to keep the ball.

"What's a first down, anyway?" Nathaniel asked.

"Gee! You really don't know much about football, do you?" Johnnie answered. Then he thought that he may have offended Nathaniel. "Sorry, I'm just so into football that I forget not everybody feels the same way."

"Oh, no offense taken!" Nathaniel said.

"Well, about that first down stuff," Johnnie said. "When a team has possession of the football, they have four chances to move it at least ten yards toward their goal. When the play stops, usually because the guy with the ball has been tackled or has been run out of bounds, then the ball is considered 'down.'

"On that last play, it was third down with five yards to go. That meant, the Warriors, had two more chances to move the ball five more yards, which they did. If they hadn't moved it five yards, then on the fourth down, they would have probably punted it back to the other team.

"But like I said, they did gain the five yards they needed, so they get to keep the ball, and now it's first down and ten yards to go—or first and ten, as the announcer would say."

"Oh! I get it! Thanks for explaining that to me. Maybe I'll be more into our football games back in Tennessee this fall!"

The clock on the scoreboard showed less than a minute of play left in the game. The Warriors were still three points ahead.

On the next play, the two teams lined up. The Warrior center held the ball on the ground between his feet. At the right signal, he snapped the ball back to the quarterback, and the entire Wildcat defensive line went into action.

The quarterback held the ball ready to pass it. His eyes scanned the field for any receivers who might be open, but there weren't any. Not wanting to be tackled, he started running with the ball toward the sidelines, but the Wildcats were there waiting for him. Then he started running back toward the Wildcat's goal, trying to keep away from the defensive team who was chasing him. By this time, it was one big chase around the field, with the time clock steadily winding down. When the scoreboard clock reached ten seconds, the fans began to count down with it:

"Ten-nine-eight-seven-all the way down to zero."

The referee blew his whistle, and the tired players stopped running around. Warrior fans cheered and jumped up and down. Wildcat fans, including Johnnie, just stood there dumbfounded. This wasn't supposed to have happened. The Wildcats were the favored team!

"Tough luck," Nathaniel said. "Why don't you and your friends meet us at the school Saturday around 9 o'clock. If your parents would like to meet us before we take off exploring, that would be fine. In fact, if some of them would like to come along, that would be great!"

"Okay!" Johnnie said. "See you on Saturday."

But his thoughts were far from exploring with the descendant of Chief Noonday. His thoughts were on next week's game. *Since we lost this week, I wonder if Coach will even let me play?*

CHAPTER 9

Ancient Treasures

Losing the first game of the season was a big disappointment to all the Wildcat fans. Travis and Danny seemed particularly dejected when they came off the field. Johnnie and the other kids went over to where the team was gathered.

"Good game!" Coach Stursma said to his players. "You all played your positions well. We'll just have to work on some defensive plays for next week's game."

Johnnie felt his heart beat faster. Would this mean the coach would want to see the special play he and the others had been practicing? Or would he want to play it "safe" and use his seasoned players?

The coach looked around at the team and then said, "Well, for those of you in my history class, you'd better forget about today's loss and study up for that test tomorrow."

A few of the players groaned. Johnnie groaned too.

Then the team headed into the locker room to shower and change out of their uniforms. Joey and Nick had to get home, but Robyn, Katy and Johnnie waited for Travis and Danny. About a half hour later, the boys emerged from the locker room, looking cleaner and more refreshed.

"Man!" Danny said. "It was so close!"

"You guys looked good out there," Johnnie commented, and the girls quickly agreed.

"Yeah, well next week will be different," Travis said.

"Do you think Coach will let us try our special play?" Johnnie asked.

"I don't know," Travis said. "But we'll keep practicing, just in case."

"Hey!" Robyn said, changing the subject. "Chief Noonday's great-great-great-oh whatever-grandson watched the game with us. *He* said that the necklace found in Johnnie's backpack was a fake!"

"What?" Danny said. "Did *you* know it was a fake?" he asked Johnnie.

Johnnie looked down at the ground not knowing what in the world he was supposed to say. "Well, I guess, since you already know it is a fake, I may as well tell you. I found out last night when Detective Knoll called my dad. I was going to say something this morning in Coach

Stursma's class, but he stopped me. Then he passed me a note saying no one was supposed to know about it."

"But Nathaniel Noonday knew about it," Robyn said.

"Yeah, I was wondering about that," Johnnie admitted. "And you know what else? He wants all of us to meet him here at 9 o'clock Saturday morning. He said he'd take us 'exploring' around Gun Lake."

"Hmm, this is very interesting," Danny remarked. "I say we go with him on Saturday and try to find out how he knew about the fake necklace."

"Maybe Detective Knoll told him, since the real one *did* belong to his ancestor," Robyn offered.

❧

Saturday morning was gray and cloudy, with just a little bit of a mist in the air. Johnnie awoke early and straightened his room. After breakfast, he told his mom that he and some of his friends were meeting Nathaniel Noonday at the school, and from there they were going to explore parts of Gun Lake.

"How well do you know this Nathaniel Noonday?" Mrs. Jacobson wanted to know.

"Hey! He came to our history class and told us some stories about Chief Noonday and the Ottawa, and then he joined us to watch the football game. He sure didn't know much about football, but he seemed eager to learn.

And he said that if you or dad or any of the parents wanted to meet him or even go along, that would be fine with him."

"Sounds like a responsible person to me," Mr. Jacobson said, glancing over the morning newspaper. "Tell you what, why don't I take you and whoever else is going, over to the school. That way I can meet Nathaniel and check him out first-hand. But I'll need to tell him that you have to be back at a certain time so I can take you home. Deal?"

"Sure!" Johnnie agreed.

≈

By 9 o'clock, all the kids were piling out of the Jacobsons' van. Nathaniel and his friends were at the school in their own van. "Hi!" Nathaniel said to Mr. Jacobson. He introduced himself and his friends. "Would you like to come with us as we do some exploring?" he asked.

"Not necessarily," Mr. Jacobson said, "unless you need some extra room to transport all these people!"

"Our van seats ten people," Nathaniel said. "And we have room in the back for Johnnie's wheelchair."

After Mr. Jacobson had talked with Nathaniel and his friends a few moments, he decided the kids would be in good hands. "I'll meet you back here around four this afternoon. Will that give you enough time to do your exploring?"

"I think that will be fine. We'll probably go into town for lunch around noon and then head back to wherever we left off," Nathaniel said. "If it should start raining, I can bring the kids home."

"Sounds good to me," Mr. Jacobson said.

ٮ

In just a matter of minutes, the kids found seats in Nathaniel's van. Johnnie, with some help from Nathaniel, was able to climb into the van and sit in the seat by the side door. His chair fit easily behind the back bench seat.

On the way to their starting point, the kids were asking their newfound friends all sorts of questions. Were they all Ottawa? Did they all live in Tennessee? What did they do for a living? On and on the questions went. And each question was answered to their satisfaction.

When the van came to a final stop, Johnnie saw that they were at the main parking lot of Yankee Springs Recreational area. "Hey! I was just here a couple weeks ago with my science class."

"And we were just here yesterday," Nathaniel said. "Some of the trails are too rough for a wheelchair, but we have rigged up a simple 'stretcher,' much like the ones the Indians used to use to transport people who were not able to walk on their own."

He pulled out a piece of canvas cloth that was stretched

between two smooth poles. "You ride in here!" Nathaniel said, pointing to the canvas.

"What? No deerskin?" Johnnie said, smiling.

"Get real!" Nathaniel joked. "Although the Ottawa were skilled at hunting and tanning deer, I'm afraid I didn't inherit that ability. We can take your wheelchair partway up the trail and just leave it there until we come back. Or, if you're afraid something will happen to it, we can leave it locked in the van."

Johnnie considered his options. "I guess I'd rather ride in my wheelchair for as long as I can," he said.

So they unloaded Johnnie's wheelchair and headed up the asphalt-covered trail. Danny offered to help Johnnie over some of the steeper hills, and Nathaniel made sure his chair didn't "run away" when it was going downhill. After about 45 minutes, they came to a narrow path.

"This is where we leave the chair and switch to the other form of transportation," Nathaniel said.

"You mean the 'stretcher,'" Johnnie said, smiling.

"Well, yeah," Nathaniel said. "But it's not like I think you're some sort of patient or anything like that."

"Ah, don't worry about it," Johnnie said. "I was just kidding around."

He pushed the wheel lock into place and proceeded to transfer out of his chair onto the "stretcher" that was placed on the ground. Once Johnnie was in the right position, Nathaniel and one of his friends, hoisted the poles up onto their shoulders. Johnnie attempted to sit up a little.

"We don't have too far to go, but it would be better if you'd lay flat, Johnnie," Nathaniel advised.

Johnnie did as he was told and enjoyed watching the sky and the tops of the trees as they wound their way into the forest. Before long, they came to a small clearing. Nathaniel and his friend carefully lowered the stretcher.

Once on the ground, Johnnie sat up and looked around. There was a large rock in a small clearing. Actually, the area looked as if it had been cleared out just recently. The morning mist was beginning to lift, and Johnnie could see the sun through the hazy sky.

"Where are we?" Johnnie asked.

"According to some ancient maps I was given, this was a very sacred place to the Ottawa who lived here," Nathaniel answered. "Many Ottawa would come here to pray or have important meetings. My friends and I came here yesterday and cleared out much of the bushes and weeds. We did some exploring in the woods but didn't really come up with anything of importance."

Suddenly, Johnnie, without thinking, blurted, "Did you bury the real Chief Noonday necklace out there?"

Nathaniel looked shocked. His two friends frowned.

Even Danny and the others looked at Johnnie in surprise.

"So, you think *I* took the necklace?" Nathaniel asked.

"How else would you have known that the one in my backpack was a fake?" Johnnie asked. "I was told that no one was supposed to know about that."

Nathaniel sighed. "I knew I had made a mistake as soon as I said that." He looked at his two friends, and they nodded.

"Yes, I took the necklace and my friends took a few other pieces of jewelry from the display. We had rigged a timing device that would cause a mini-blackout so the lights would go off. During the time the lights were out, I was going to take Noonday's necklace and replace it with a fake one. My other two friends here decided to take the other pieces of jewelry too. I had both necklaces in my hand when the lights flickered back on—faster than I had thought they would. So now I was stuck with *two* necklaces. I was standing near you, Johnnie, and saw your open backpack. Without thinking, I dropped the fake one in your backpack—or so I thought."

It was Johnnie's turn to look shocked. "What? You mean that was the *real* necklace in my backpack?"

"Yes! When I realized my mistake, I threw the fake one away in disgust," Nathaniel said.

"And the police must have found it," Katy said, her

eyes sparkling with excitement. "Then they knew that the thief would come after the real necklace!"

She looked quickly at Nathaniel and said, "Oh, I'm sorry. I didn't mean to call you a thief."

"Well, I guess I am," Nathaniel said. "Anyway, we brought the other pieces of jewelry here yesterday, and placed them under this rock."

"Why are you telling us all this?" Travis asked. "Are you going to hurt us or something?"

"Oh, no, no, no!" Nathaniel answered. "We had a long talk yesterday, trying to figure out what to do. The only reason we took the necklace in the first place is because it really belongs to the Ottawa people. A lot of our pottery, jewelry and other items were taken to Europe by the settlers. I know it's illegal to do that now, but back then, some of our most beautiful and priceless items were taken and have ended up in European museums, like the one in Great Britain."

"So, to your way of thinking, you were merely taking back what you thought rightfully belonged to you?" Robyn asked.

"Yes. I thought I'd have enough time to replace the necklace, and then no one would even know the difference. It's made out of real copper and the fabric is as close to authentic as you can get. I just wanted the real one my ancestor had worn."

"So, I ask again," Travis said. "Why did you bring us all the way out here to tell us that? You could have said something back at the school."

"Let me guess! Let me guess!" Katy was so excited she bounced around the "sacred ground" like a kangaroo. "You wanted us to 'discover' these treasures under that rock and take them back to the police."

"Very good!" Nathaniel said, obviously impressed.

"So why did you tell us about everything instead of letting us find the treasures?" Travis wondered.

Nathaniel sat on the ground next to the rock. "I really thought we could pull it off. And then Johnnie just comes out and asks that question. I *knew* I had made a big mistake at the school when I mentioned the fake necklace. I thought I could keep your mind off it, Johnnie, by asking all the football questions. But you weren't fooled.

"It was kind of a dumb plan anyway," he continued. "I guess, my friends and I just want to turn ourselves in and be done with it."

Everyone was quiet for a while. "Well, let's see what's under the rock," Joey said. And everyone laughed.

They dug up some small pieces of beaded jewelry and a cloth scarf that was hand dyed. "Well, maybe we could tell everyone that we found these..." Johnnie began.

"No!" Nathaniel said. "That would make this an even bigger wrong. It would make all of you a part of the crime."

He sat there a while and then picked up all the items they had dug up. "By the time we get back to the van it will be afternoon. Let's head back to Gun Lake and get something to eat. I'll take you guys home, and then my friends and I will head over to the police station."

Nathaniel started to get up when Johnnie placed his hand on his leg. "I'm sorry," Johnnie said. "I'm sorry your plan didn't work. I wish you could have taken back Chief Noonday's necklace."

Nathaniel smiled, his dark eyes gleaming. "Thanks, Johnnie!"

CHAPTER 10

The Game

The town of Gun Lake was buzzing with the news about the stolen Ottawa artifacts being turned in. Johnnie and his family watched the evening news where pictures of Nathaniel and his friends were shown along with photos of Chief Noonday's necklace and the other things they took that day. A spokesman for the museum said how glad they were to have the articles back.

"I realize these young descendants of Chief Noonday thought they had a right to these items, but the jewelry didn't even belong to us at the museum. They were on loan to us from the British Museum, and we were very concerned that this could cause some sort of international problem," the man said.

The arrest of Nathaniel Noonday and his friends brought on a small uprising from the Ottawa people who still resided in West Michigan. And their protests found support among many people who believed Native American artifacts belonged in the United States not in foreign countries.

"I talked with Detective Knoll this afternoon," Mr. Jacobson said. "Apparently there is a very well-known attorney from New York who wants to defend Nathaniel. You know, he faces charges of grand larceny."

"Grand what?" Johnnie asked.

"Larceny," Mr. Jacobson repeated. "It's just a fancy word for *theft*."

"And *grand* larceny means it was worth a lot of money," Mrs. Jacobson added.

"I feel bad for Nathaniel," Johnnie said. "He did it because he believed it was the right thing to do. Doesn't that count for something?"

"Well, I can certainly understand *why* he did it," Mr. Jacobson said. "But breaking the law isn't right, even when we think we're doing it for a good reason."

"What do you think will happen?" Johnnie asked.

"Well, there will be a hearing, and a lot depends on how Nathaniel and his friends plead—you know, guilty or not guilty. I think it helps that everything was returned and that they turned themselves in. Plus, I hear that New York lawyer is pretty good. He's part Chippewa himself!"

❧

The next morning was Sunday. Danny called Johnnie

in the afternoon. "Hey!" he said. "We'd better get some football practice in. The game is this Thursday!"

"Okay," Johnnie said. "I'll meet you at the park in an hour."

❧

Johnnie's dad dropped Johnnie and his crutches off. "Do you mind if I watch?" he asked.

Johnnie looked a little uncomfortable. "We're sort of practicing this 'secret game plan,' Dad, if you know what I mean. You could come to the game Thursday night. We're playing at the high school—under the lights!"

Mr. Jacobson smiled. "Well, okay. I guess I'll just have to wait to find out what this 'secret' play of yours is! I'll come back in a couple hours to pick you up!" With that he waved goodbye as he drove off.

Johnnie watched him go. "Hey! Johnnie! Are you going to play or are you going to watch the traffic go by?" Travis yelled at him from the field.

Johnnie laid his crutches across his lap and started pushing his wheelchair toward the field. Danny and the others were already there warming up. "Do some laps around the walkway," Travis ordered.

Johnnie dropped his crutches on the ground and then pushed off toward the asphalt walkway. He managed to get in about five laps when Travis called the team together.

"All right, Johnnie, I'm the center, and you have to make it so the others can get past me to the quarterback, which is Danny. So, Joey, Nick and Johnnie, you line up as the defensive line. Me, Robyn and Katy are the offensive line."

Johnnie's heart was pounding. "Okay," he said to himself, "I *have* to make this work."

⁂

They spent the afternoon perfecting their play. Just before they were going to call it quits, they noticed Coach Stursma standing to one side of the bleachers.

"Coach!" Johnnie cried. "How long have you been standing there?"

The coach began walking toward the players. "Well, I've been standing here long enough to understand what your special play is," he said. "I'm not so sure that it will work against a real offensive line—no offense girls. But I do have to admit, it's got possibilities. Tomorrow, after school, I want you to suit up and join us for practice, Johnnie. If you can hold up during regular practice, then maybe I'll let you play in the game on Thursday."

"Yes!" Johnnie cried. "I'll be there, and you'll see, Coach. It *will* work."

⁂

Johnnie had a difficult time focusing on schoolwork

that Monday. All he could think about was proving himself during football practice. When the sky clouded up around lunchtime, Johnnie thought he'd go crazy. "If it's just a drizzling rain, they'll still have practice," he reminded himself. "But if there's thunder, then no way!"

Just then, there was a loud KA-BOOM! Johnnie nearly jumped out of his chair. "Was that thunder?" he yelled. Heads turned toward him as if he were crazy.

"No," Danny said, as he sat down next to Johnnie. "That was definitely *not* thunder. It sounded like someone dropped one of those big kettles in the kitchen. Boy, are you uptight or what!"

Johnnie grinned sheepishly. "Okay, maybe I'm just a little nervous. You would be nervous too if you had to pull off this play of ours."

"Yeah, I guess I would be," Danny admitted. "But don't worry. You really did great out there yesterday, and despite what Coach says, Robyn and Katy are probably as tough as most of the offensive lines in middle school football. Plus, it wasn't *them* you were tackling. It was Mr. Football himself, Travis Hughes!"

ॐ

Finally school was over. Johnnie went into the locker room and began getting into his uniform. He strapped on his shoulder pads and made sure the thigh and hip pads were in the correct inside pockets of the uniform's pants. Coach Stursma came up to him and handed him the standard helmet and faceguard.

"You have a mouthpiece, I assume?" Coach asked.

"Yep! I bought one Saturday and molded it to my mouth size right away. Last year's was a little beat up," Johnnie said.

Johnnie warmed up with the rest of the team, and then got ready for the "big" play. Coach didn't waste any time getting to it either. Without telling the offensive line what was going on, he filled in the defensive team.

They looked at Coach Stursma with surprise. Then they looked at Johnnie. The words "you've got to be kidding me" were written on their faces.

"Don't knock it until you've tried it," Coach said.

The offensive team lined up first. Then Johnnie walked to his position, using his crutches. The center on the offensive line looked puzzled. "Just do your job, Brian," Coach yelled to the center player.

What took place in the next few seconds was nothing short of spectacular. When the play was all over, the center looked up from the ground and said, "Hey, coach? Was that legal?"

Coach Stursma smiled. "You bet! There is nothing—and I mean *nothing*—in the rule books that would stop this play. But it still needs some work. Let's try it again."

Johnnie was pumped. And at the end of practice, Coach told him to show up for *every* practice.

❧

Meanwhile, during that week, Nathaniel Noonday's attorney was busily hammering out a deal with the prosecutor's office. And, it was learned, the Grand Rapids museum had made an offer to purchase Chief Noonday's necklace. So far the British weren't budging, however.

"Can't they see it belongs here?" Johnnie asked Coach Stursma, after class on Thursday.

"Whether they see that or not is not the point," Coach Stursma said. "They feel they have ownership of the necklace, and if someone wants it, well, they are going to have to pay a big price to get it."

"That just doesn't seem right, somehow," Johnnie argued. "I heard that Nathaniel and his friends may get out on bail. Is that true?"

"Could be," Coach Stursma said. "But for right now, I think you should be concentrating first, on your schoolwork for today and second, on the game this evening."

Johnnie smiled. "Yeah, I guess you're right."

❧

After school, Johnnie was so jittery he could hardly eat dinner. Mrs. Jacobson had made a light dinner for 5 o'clock, so Johnnie would have plenty of time to get to the high school. He arrived there at six that evening, along with the rest of the team.

Coach Stursma gave them the usual pep talk and then had them do some warm-ups as they waited for 7:00 p.m. to roll around. As the team went out onto the field to do stretches, Johnnie saw the stands were filling up fast. He scanned the bleachers to see if he could find his family. Already, the big stadium lights were lit. Just then he saw his dad and mom standing up waving wildly at him. He smiled, made sure no one on his team was looking, and gave a small wave back. His sisters Corry and Elsa were there too, he noticed.

"You all ready for tonight?" Danny asked, as he came up behind where Johnnie was sitting on the team's bench.

"I'm as ready as I'll ever be," Johnnie said. "I just wish we'd hurry up and get started."

"Yeah, me too," Danny said.

❧

Before long, it was the opening kick off. The Wildcats were hosts to the Trailblazers, a team that was a pretty even match. During the first quarter of the game, the Wildcats managed to score a touchdown and an extra point, making the score 7-0. The second quarter ended with no one scoring.

Johnnie sat on the sidelines with the team during the halftime entertainment. "Hey, Coach," one of the players yelled out, "when are you going to let Johnnie play?"

Johnnie was grateful someone else had asked the question that was foremost on his mind.

"I'm putting him in during the fourth quarter," Coach said. Then he went on talking to the team about strategy, being a team player, and playing their hardest.

The third quarter whistle blew. The Trailblazers came back onto the field with determination burning in their eyes. They had possession of the ball. On the first play, their quarterback dropped back, looking for a receiver. Finally, his wide receiver broke free, and the quarterback threw a long pass straight into the receiver's hands. When he had a good grip on the ball, he started running down the sideline toward the goal. Touchdown! After the extra point was kicked, the score was tied, 7-7. Try as they might, neither team could score again, and the quarter ended in a tie.

Then, during the first play of the fourth quarter the Trailblazers tried another long pass down the field. It looked like one of their receivers was going to catch it, when a Wildcat safety ran in front of the receiver, jumped up and caught the ball. He dodged several Trailblazer offensive players, who tried to tackle him. Eventually he twisted and turned his way down to the 15-yard line. Now it was the Wildcat's ball.

On the first play, Travis tried to pass it to Danny, but the ball was high and Danny couldn't reach it. On the second play, Travis handed the ball to the halfback, but he was almost immediately tackled. Now it was third down and still nine yards to go. When the ball was snapped to the quarterback, Danny ran into the end zone. Travis spotted him. Just then a Trailblazer defensive linebacker managed to break through the line and tackled Travis, who still had the ball in his hand. Travis hit the ground hard but managed to tuck the ball safely under him, so he wouldn't fumble it.

There was no other choice. It was fourth down, and it was unlikely that the Wildcats could score a touchdown. So, the kicker came out onto the field. The center hiked the ball to Travis. He held it steady for the kicker, whose foot made solid contact with the ball. It sailed high and straight between the goal posts. A field goal—worth three points! And the score was now Wildcats, 10; Trailblazers, 7.

"Okay, Johnnie," Coach said. "Here's your chance! Do it just like we did in practice."

Using his crutches, Johnnie walked as fast as he could onto the field and got into position.

"Go Johnnie!" Robyn and Katy yelled.

"It's the secret play! It's the secret play!" Joey screamed, jumping up and down.

Johnnie's parents were also in the stands watching their son walk out onto the field. "Oh, I can't look," Mrs. Jacobson said.

"Come on, he'll be fine," Mr. Jacobson reassured her. "You're going to miss the greatest play of the entire game if you keep your face buried in my shoulder like that!

Reluctantly, she peeked at the field and kept her eyes fixed on her son, while maintaining a firm grip on her husband's jacket.

Other spectators murmured things like, "What's he doing?"

"What's with the crutches?"

"Who is *that*?"

With his crutches supporting him, Johnnie faced the Trailblazers' center lineman. The lineman looked up at him with a puzzled look on his face.

"Oh, I've seen *that* look before," Johnnie said, a mischievous smile on his face. "Just remember, I'm your worst nightmare."

When the center snapped the ball back to his quarterback, Johnnie dropped his crutches and literally threw his body forward onto the center's back. This, of course, caused the center to fall down and, with the center out of the way, opened up a hole for the other defensive players to run through and go for the quarterback. The surprised quarterback dropped the ball but immediately fell on it.

The Wildcat cheering section went wild! The Trailblazers suffered a loss of eight yards, and it was now second and 18. After two more tries, the Trailblazers couldn't move the ball more than nine yards, and so they had to kick it away to the Wildcats.

The Wildcats maintained possession of the ball for quite a while, slowly moving it down the field. But they just couldn't get it into the end zone. Then, during a fourth down pass, Travis threw the ball into the outstretched hands of a Trailblazer player. An interception! The player was immediately tackled at the Wildcat's 21-yard line.

Coach Stursma put Johnnie back into the game. As he did before, Johnnie dropped his crutches and lunged forward, which was very effective. However, the Trailblazers managed to scoot the ball forward for a first down. Time was critical at this point, with only 2 minutes and 39 seconds left on the game clock.

It was the Trailblazer's job to get the ball, if not into the end zone, at least close enough so their kicker could try for a field goal and tie the score. And it was the Wildcats' job to stop them.

The Trailblazers worked hard and managed to move the ball over the 50-yard line. The two-minute warning sounded, and the Trailblazers called a time out.

Back at the Wildcat sideline, Coach Stursma was pacing back and forth. "You've got to stop them," he said. "I'm going to keep Johnnie in the game. Okay, guys, let's play some defensive football out there!"

When the players ran back onto the field, there was exactly two minutes left to play. Johnnie lined up nose to nose with the center, and while he managed to tackle him, the quarterback was able to hand off the ball to their halfback. The boy ran up the field, only to be met by the Wildcat defensive line. So he ran sideways toward the sidelines but couldn't get out of bounds. Then he started running back toward his own goal. By running around the field, he used up 18 seconds.

The Trailblazer coach signaled for a time out, just as the clocked showed 1 minute, 42 seconds left in the game. When the Trailblazers came back onto the field and lined up, Johnnie was there, looking at the center, who had a strange little smile on *his* face.

The quarterback called out the signals and the center snapped the ball. But as soon as the football was out of his hands, he quickly stood up. Johnnie saw that he wouldn't be able to jump on the center's back, so he dropped to the ground, grabbed his opponent's ankles and pulled. The momentum of the center standing up quickly and Johnnie pulling his feet out from under him caused the center to actually flip back and land on his own quarterback! The quarterback, who was totally unprepared for this, lost his grip on the football. But instead of the ball hitting the ground, it went straight up in the air—and into the hands of a Wildcat defensive player, who actually ran over Johnnie and the center in order to catch it.

It was all over for the Trailblazers from there. The stands erupted in yelling and applause.

Mrs. Jacobson jumped to her feet and yelled, "That's my son out there! That's my Johnnie!" Mr. Jacobson beamed with pride, and laughed at his wife's newfound excitement over football.

Fans could hardly wait for the game to be over so they could rush onto the field and congratulate the players.

"That was one awesome play!" said a familiar voice, as Johnnie sat on the bench. He turned to see the smiling face of Nathaniel Noonday.

"Hey cool!" Johnnie said. "They let you out!"

"Yep! Some of my Ottawa friends here posted bail for us and have even given us a place to stay until this is all over," Nathaniel said. "And as long as I was out, I thought I'd see what this famous play of yours was all about. I have to admit, you were pretty spectacular! I wonder if they do any of that sort of stuff in the pros?"

Johnnie laughed. "I doubt it."

Nathaniel's face became serious. "You're a real inspiration to me, Johnnie. You had something you really wanted to do—something important to you, and you found a way—a right way, I might add—to do it. I believe my cause of retrieving Native American artifacts from other countries is important too. And I intend to pursue that—but in a *right* way, not a wrong way."

Johnnie smiled.

Just then Coach Stursma came up, grinning broadly. "What a game! That was a great play out there!"

Johnnie was about to open his mouth and say something, when he heard a loud, high-pitched, "Jo—hn—i—eeee!"

From out of the bleachers, Mrs. Swanson, the lunch lady, came bounding across the field, the ends of her frizzy red hair flying about in a frenzy. She practically knocked Coach Stursma off his feet as she plopped herself down on the bench beside Johnnie.

"Oh, Johnnie!" she said. Her cheeks were all red and she was breathing hard from running across the field. "I'm so proud of you!" And she reached over and gave him a big hug.

Johnnie was surprised by her hug but even more surprised by the tears he saw in her eyes.

"You are simply too much! And to think I wouldn't let you eat spaghetti! Well, next week, I'm going to make sure you have the biggest plate of spaghetti ever served at Gun Lake Middle School!"

She gave Johnnie one last hug and ran off.

"What was *that* all about?" Coach wanted to know.

Danny, who had watched the whole scene from a safe distance began to laugh. "Oh, it's a Johnnie thing," he said. "He just does that to people."

Johnnie smiled and shrugged. "Yeah, I guess I do!"

A portion of the proceeds from sales of The Gun Lake Adventure Series goes to support the nonprofit organization Alternatives in Motion, founded by Johnnie Tuitel in 1995. The mission of Alternatives in Motion is to provide wheelchairs to individuals who do not qualify for other assistance and who could not obtain such equipment without financial aid.

For further information or to make donations, please contact Johnnie Tuitel at:

Alternatives in Motion
1916 Breton Rd. S.E.
Grand Rapids, MI 49506
(616) 493-2620 (voice)
(616) 493-2621 (fax)

Alternatives in Motion is a nonprofit 501(c)(3) organization.

www.alternativesinmotion.org

Gun Lake
Adventure Series

From the Midwest Book Review:

"...A pure delight for young readers, *Discovery on Blackbird Island* is the third volume in "The Gun Lake Adventure Series" and like its predecessors, *The Barn at Gun Lake* and *Mystery Explosion!*, showcases the substantial storytelling talents of Johnnie Tuitel and Sharon Lamson."

From Early On Michigan Newsletter:

"This little book is a gem."

From Pooh's Corner Bookstore:

"The *Gun Lake Adventure* series provides action, adventure, fun and friends...elements kids love to read about."

From the Grand Rapids Press:

"...(the) Gun Lake Adventure Series is capturing the attention of young readers in Grand Rapids and beyond."

From WE Magazine:

"An excellent venture."

by Johnnie Tuitel and Sharon Lamson.

The Barn at Gun Lake (1998, Cedar Tree Publishing, $5.99 paperback, **Book 1**)
The Gun Lake kids stumble upon a cadre of modern pirates when they find an illegal copy of a popular CD in a deserted barn. While solving the mystery, there is a boat chase and then a harrowing wheelchair chase through the woods. This story is great reading adventure.

Mystery Explosion! (1999, Cedar Tree Publishing, $5.99 paperback, **Book 2**)
First there is an explosion. Then an arrest is made that shocks the quiet town of Gun Lake. A stranger in town, and a search for his identity, paves the way for another fast-paced mystery. Friendships and loyalties are tested as Johnnie Jacobson and the kids try to find the answers to "Who did it?" and "Why?"

Discovery on Blackbird Island (2000, Cedar Tree Publishing, $5.99 paperback, **Book 3**)
Blackbird Island — a small, quiet uninhabited island in Gun Lake — isn't what it appears to be. A disturbing discovery sends Johnnie Jacobson and his friends on yet another Gun Lake adventure filled with schemes, action and mysteries to solve.

For more information or distribution contact:
Tap Shoe Productions, Inc.
888-302-7463   www.tapshoe.com

Books in the Gun Lake Adventure Series

For yong readers aged 8-12, Children/Juvenile $5.99

For more information contact: Tap Shoe Productions.
1916 Breton Road S.E., Grand Rapids, MI 49506
tel: 616-831-0030, toll free: 888-302-7463
fax: 616-493-2621, www.tapshoe.com